FABLES

FABLES

Sarah Goldstein

:: TARPAULIN SKY PRESS ::
:: GRAFTON, VERMONT ::

Fables
© 2011 Sarah Goldstein

First Edition, May 2011
ISBN: 978-0-9825416-6-1

Printed and bound in the USA.

Library of Congress Control Number: 2010941883

Tarpaulin Sky Press
P.O. Box 189
Grafton, Vermont 05146
www.tarpaulinsky.com

For more information on Tarpaulin Sky Press perfect-bound and
hand-bound editions, as well as information regarding distribution,
personal orders, and catalogue requests, please visit our website at
www.tarpaulinsky.com.

For Joshua

CONTENTS

GRIM

She had to dance till she was dead on the ground. She was turned into a lake. Her sweetheart was turned into a duck.

She can see the wind, red and vengeful, coming up the street. The poodle dog eats coals and his throat catches fire. I should like to have a bird such as sings like that, she says, and her sweetheart brings the bird down with a bow and arrow.

FABLES

I.

Many old wives' tales persist in town, such as: *take an orphan child hunting, you will return with threefold the bounty*. Although law forbids observing such advice, a hard winter is coming. Some adults decide to take a few of these unfortunate children into the woods. The hunt yields nothing. After several days, the adults become frustrated, and the already grief-stricken children know something is wrong. Sunlight fails through the tree canopy, and the children see ever more owls and bats. They sneak away from the hunting party and wander the forest. Nightjars and swifts circle, alight on their arms, pinch them. Swallows dive and take tufts of their hair. Exhausted, the children crawl into the undergrowth. They feel safe and sleep, but wake without memory of themselves. When they cry, it is the sounds of the whippoorwills. The nightingales become their mothers, and pheasants usher them to winter quarters. Meanwhile, the adults have returned to town to face the others. Everyone grimaces, hearing only what they decide to understand.

2.

The girl comes clambering up the hill from the meadow
to the house, whispering the message into her hands.
Now the sheep in the field, the holes in the ground; and
she stops, having entered the kitchen. Her mother is
on the floor in the corner, curled with her fingers in
her mouth. The rabbit her father tossed on the counter
for stew has awakened, and they watch as it lurches
towards the window. Outside, the dogs begin to howl
and their father comes into the kitchen. He holds his
shovel like a sword, breathing heavily. In the barn, the
cats are stalking the mice they killed that morning,
mice that now stagger across the rough-hewn floors.

They caught nothing that day, and finally the hunters turned for home. In daylight the trail was wide enough, but at dusk they felt encircled by bare branches, leaning trunks, hidden eyes. One hunter started to cough and his eyes burned. Another incessantly scratched at his hands, his arms, and felt his toes growing swollen inside his sodden boots. The third stopped outright and began tearing at his hair, crying out that his scalp was burning. Their breath steamed around them in the cold early twilight; no wind came up to whisk it away. Each stumbled and rasped, feeling out for the others but unable to find them. Finally their cries became less intelligible. The man with the burning scalp raised his head and looked around him, but all he saw was a hare thrashing about to his left and a buck struggling to its feet on his right. "My gun!" he cried, but he heard only grunts. His mouth felt full of gravel and his teeth ground together like ball bearings. The buck began to cry and rammed itself into a tree, while the hare turned to flee from the boar lurching toward it, unsteady and reeling.

4.

They call him hatchet-head, spoon-nose, moon-face. His friends are a worn-out bicycle and the family dog, who is graying and slow. They barely endure his talking at home, and his mother frequently buries small talismans in the backyard after his father has gone to bed. One night she falls asleep in the yard, and wakes to find her son holding a bouquet of fiddleheads, puffballs, and sumac. She feels very hot, as though the sun is out. But it is only that the moon has risen to a brightness she no longer anticipates, and she hears the river recede into its rocky bed. Her son's face is nodding and difficult to see, yellow in a blurring glow.

5.

Not so long ago the crops were terrible, and the farmer came home each night worried and wondering how to keep going. Usually there were chickens and rabbits for his wife to cook, but not anymore: now they are almost out of everything. The wife opens her window and lays out a few crumbs of bread on the sill as she has every day for the past several years. The sparrows come, heads cocked. In return for the crumbs, they have cleaned her bushes of centipedes, crickets, and biting spiders. They hear her whisper, see the trail laid out for them. That night the farmer returns to a better meal than usual, crunches down the stringy, bone-ridden bits in the stew. Strange, but satisfying, he tells her, before going to bed. She stays up a bit longer by the dying cinders, fingers tapping the rhythms of birdsong. Her insides are fluttering with the beats of tiny organs, there's something stuck in her throat, and her eyes are wide and barely blinking.

6.

After enduring many years of abuse, the children decide to do away with their father. With some effort they manage to turn him out of the house like a sack of flour. Before dawn comes they must heave him to the field and bury him, although one girl suggests a burned corpse is harder to identify. They enlist some spiteful friends to help, but only after bribes of candy and their father's remaining stash of cigarettes and liquor. Everyone's chest is indented with cowardice and sorrow by daylight. At school that day some of them kill a toad and leave it on the teacher's chair. When no one confesses all are made to sit, palms up, to receive the lashing. Laughter cuts the otherwise silent classroom in between the cracking of rulers.

7.

You and I have an agreement, don't we? We shall cross the country by foot and sleep in the barns and cabins of unsuspecting city folk who are away until the weekend. Or we will find shelter in garages, through unlocked cellar doors, maybe curl up together in blankets on beds of leaves, pine needles, under hemlocks. Each day we will move just beyond sight of the highways, we will forge new trails at the edges of farmers' fields, we will steal apples from the orchards and cream from the vats in the milking sheds. These parts of the economy sputter onward, but the cities are dying. Better to make this our new life, embrace it, than rot in spirit and body in the embers of the crumbling urban commerce. To see the rabbit slung across your shoulder as you return from the hunt is all the retirement plan I will ever require.

8.

The town is definitely cursed, but some decide to stay there anyway. They watch their screens carefully to help figure out where to burn the leftover parts. They should not forget their protectors, they say to one another. They should remember to chlorinate the water and bathe every third day. The women can be assembled in one area to watch the food. It'll work itself out once the clouds blow away to the east. The screens have a steady flickering pattern that interferes with live broadcasts of unsmiling, wide-shouldered men in heavy suits. The dogs of the town lie in a heap and cough, shuddering with every breath.

9.

The two men were cast off several days ago in a small boat with no oars, motor, or sail. Now the sun is quite high, and they grow weak, huddled miserably under a tarp. They stare at each other's tumescent faces, bruises under their eyes, cut lips and cheeks. One of them is still shackled at his ankle. Suddenly the boat bumps against something. They peer into the water: it is thick with waving weeds and rubbish. They see bits of clothing floating up, hands, feet, and pale faces rubbed clean and characterless by the deep water. And thus do the various offspring of their murderous lives begin to clamber over the sides of the boat, swollen and silent.

10.

They have been planning the switch for months. The girls grow their hair and dye it the same pale blonde, start buying and wearing identical shapeless dresses, apply their makeup in the same technique and palette. Some kids think it's cool, but others avoid them because it's so strange. At first they swap places in a few of their classes to see if the teachers might notice, but none do. Soon afterwards they go to each other's houses after school, eat dinner with the other's equally chaotic family, and stay the night in the other's bed. Each room has the other girl's scent and pattern of disorder. Each lies awake in a strange house, unsure of the night noises and constituent conversations. At school the next day they congratulate each other on their deception. And so it continues: the two families, inconsistent and self-centered, never catch on. One day one of the girls does not show up at school. In fact, she is never seen again, since the entire family has fled in the night to avoid their many debts. A letter finally arrives for the abandoned girl, postmarked from another country, with pictures of a new house, an ocean. "I love them and have left myself," she reads, "I left myself so long ago, please, don't be angry."

II.

The young man shoots the deer, grabs its head, and thrusts his face down so his mouth and nose are just touching the animal's snout, where small drops of blood and foam have flecked. The deer is too weak to struggle, and as its last gasps of breath ease out, the man inhales them sharply. His eyes blur and he feels faint, releasing the deer and sinking down beside it. Cursed blood roils his body, and he presses hard on his own chest to stop the wild hammering.

12.

The young couple is growing anxious. The creaking floors above them are getting too loud to ignore. She rubs her temples until the bone appears, and he wears all his ties at once. They throw poisoned bread up into the attic and quickly shut the door. They hear something thrashing, moaning, spinning in agony, so violent that cracks appear in the ceiling. Dragging it out to the backyard the next night proves difficult. Doorways are sawed apart, every piece of linen in the house is enlisted to wrap and sop. Outside, they see curious raccoons and deer gathered in the brief sweep of the flashlights—drawn by what, she can't imagine. Her bandaged head is throbbing. Their garage fills with smoke.

13.

They have been banned from the local swimming pool and their parents complained about the trenches they dug in their backyards, so the three girls meet in the colorless dawn by the pond near the highway. People in the cars going by seem not to notice. The girls hold each other's hands and wade into the shallowest part of the pond, shivering violently. They kneel down and take turns inhaling the stagnant, rusty-tasting wetness, the microbes and the dirt. Now they cannot be seen from the road at all. Each day they return to practice their underwater breathing. When it does flood the following month, they laugh and swim gloriously between submerged houses like underage mermaids, lithe among bloated debris.

14.

The stable boy was a little vain, but he never beat the horses. Then he stupidly left the gate open and spilled all the oats on the ground. A stag leapt in and began to eat the oats with relish. Two crows perched on the fence, hoping for leftovers. "Remember that we scream to warn you when the hunters get too close!" they said. The stag refused to let them eat, so the crows flew away in disgust. They complained to the fox and she vowed to help them get revenge. The fox crept down to the barn and sneaked inside. She grabbed a piglet from its pen and ran with it, squealing and kicking, in her mouth up to the horse's enclosure. The washerwoman heard the commotion and yelled for the stable boy and head groom. They came running with rifles and followed the fox. The crows flew over the stag and set upon him, flapping around his antlers while the terrified horses ran to the far side of the field. When the stable boy came upon the stag and the crows, he steadied himself and aimed his rifle. The stag fell on the first shot, and the crows headed for the trees while the fox disappeared into the briar bushes with the piglet. Now the stable boy is even more proud of himself, as there is venison tonight for the servants. At dinner the stable boy gets drunk and asks the chambermaid to dance, and such a rowdy night follows that they are all docked a day's wages. The crows look in vain for the fox with her tender piglet. The horses roll their eyes at every sound and stay very still as the late stars pass away into a purplish new sky.

Every day a group of volunteers heads into one of the neighborhood quadrants. Each has a backpack with supplies and keeps the flyers at hand at all times. The flyer is printed in four languages, but if nobody at the house speaks one of those languages then the volunteers must mark the door for the cadets. If no one answers the door but the door is unlocked, the volunteers can go inside. They take a few pictures and write short lines down on a clipboard. They encounter abandoned pets, piles of garbage, and, once in a while, elderly or infirm occupants who remain. One house contained only children who hid when the volunteers entered and would not re-emerge. The questions most likely to be asked of the volunteers are written on the back of the clipboard. "When will the electricity be turned back on?" (Answer: "Your electric supplier is working on the problem and expects power to be back on soon!") "Where can I go to get medical help?" (Answer: "Register at the city police department between 9 A.M. and 5 P.M. and wait for further instructions.") In the event that a volunteer discharges a firearm, the quadrant manager signs off on the yellow form for the dispatch director. At the end of the week, the manager with the fewest firearm discharges gets an extra half-day off and a free package of waterproof matches.

16.

The goat was found hanging by its neck, just a few inches above the ground. The farmer's wife was inconsolable because the goat gave them milk every day and ate the sharp-tipped weeds around her garden. The farmer found his son, whose job it was to watch the goat, and knocked him about with a rake. The son ran to the neighbor's field and tried to become a hermit. He burrowed into a foxhole and glared out at the world. By nightfall all the foxes and coyotes in the valley came to taunt him. "Goat-hanger," they cried, "what a psycho!" The son claimed the goat had nibbled off his toe while he slept, but he'd actually caught a fishhook in it, and it rotted off on its own. In a few days he was starving, and when he crawled out of the hole the foxes held him down while the coyotes tore his tongue out. They didn't want to hear his lies anymore.

17.

Three boys decide to go into the pine forest together. The carpet of needles is thick and they barely make a sound as they walk. After several hours of hiking they find what used to be the house. Now it is a blackened frame among piles of partly burned garbage and rusted car parts. At the back are the charred remains of two horses that were tied to a tree. The boys twist and pry some of the hooves off the carcasses and head for home, but as darkness falls they become lost. The hooves smell terrible and weigh heavily in the boy's pockets, so they throw them to the ground in disgust. They spend the night in the forest and their clothes stink of rot. In the morning the search party finds them, retching and pale by a stream. Weeks after they have returned home, the doctors can find nothing wrong with the boys except for the awful stench that won't go away. One of them has singed all of the hair from his arms and legs and shaved his head; another takes scalding hot baths several times a day and much of the skin has peeled from his body. The boys sometimes search the pine forest for the place where they threw the hooves away. In this dim and dappled landscape the shapes of horses converge and disappear around them with maddening regularity.

18.

A pack of dogs, well ahead of the hunters, treed the bear quickly. Utterly enraged by his predicament, the bear tore off pieces of himself and threw them to the dogs. This only increased their frenzy, and as the bear grew angrier he simply threw more of his body down below. When the hunters finally arrived, the bloody bear slipped from the tree, now just a drape of fur and sinew, bone and claws. The dogs frothed, tails tucked, sucking marrow and gagging hide. The silent hunters held rifles up, but what readiness warrants against a shadow of a bear such as this? They all watched his breath whistle away. When they rubbed their eyes it was a pink night edging the dull sky, dogs choking and pitching beside them for the long walk home.

Browning flowers bend along the driveway of a
medium-sized white house. The man who lives there
marries every few years, taking a new young bride who
subsequently drives away in the night, or who vanishes
on her way to the grocery store, or dies in childbirth
along with the infant. The neighbors hear no fighting;
in fact, they barely see anyone about the property at all.
Yet each winter weak plumes of brown smoke etch out
of the chimney, and someone prunes back the bushes
in early spring. The man in the house is observant, for
he counts and measures the boot prints in the snow.
He knows which are his, which are the meter reader's,
and which are those of the curious children who circle
the house in the night, until he chases them like rabbits
from the undergrowth with an old cane switch.

20.

At dusk one day a finch flew into the kitchen of a lazy woman and her daughter. They trapped her inside for the night and gave her a piece of lace to finish mending, then some torn underwear, and then a delicate handkerchief with frayed edges. The finch nipped and hopped and pulled and handled the needle with ease. Finally they gave her a heavy black coat with fine white stitching that had come apart, and urged her to fix it. The finch did as they asked, for she feared she would never be let go if she refused. Then she sank down, exhausted, as it was nearing dawn. The mother and daughter turned to each other and blushed, suddenly ashamed that they made the finch work so hard. They lit the copper pot to serve her some tea. But it was too late: the bird was dead. While the sun rose, the women were framed in the window with the morning light, averting their eyes and stroking the finch, hoping to coax her alive. When they did glance into the sun coming into the kitchen, a crow flew by the window, and in that black second they both lost their sight forever. Now they stumble about the cold house, fighting over the old coat the dead finch mended for them.

21.

All the Birds of Finland. Smoke trapped in the attic. The boy holds illustrations up to the window and traces bird bodies onto sheets of paper towel. *Corvus corax.* Feral cats caught in traps, blood on canvas, mice in laundry baskets, passerines, tail feathers, sky without color. Grasping a pencil with his small hands, imagining the miles of territory they must cover. Paper towel birds lined neatly in rows, eyes sketched in with water drops.

His father dreams of chivalrous men dancing with beautiful women, slowly spinning. Empty light sockets on the front porch became clogged with nests, punched out with broom ends, all crap and feathers. The car's backseat holds only empty soda cans never redeemed.

22.

Everyone agreed it was a freak accident: the father in the yellow house caught his unkempt hair in the axle of the truck he was underneath, replacing some part or another; rusty jacks holding up the vehicle gave way when he tried to yank himself free. Later: dogs with bloody hair in their mouths; the police who simply wrote it all down; a hollow quiet that embraced the street for months afterward. Nobody spoke, lest it be broken.

23.

With this you'll be able to sew together anything you find, the witch said: such a tiny needle and it still left her with bloody fingers. For a year she was the most prosperous seamstress in the village. Then the needle ran away, and she could not earn a penny. Her husband circled the house with the axe on his shoulder, shouting for her to come outside. She froze, listening for his footsteps to fade away. When evening came, she climbed a small tree and sat down. The next day and for many days afterward she searched for the needle until her hunger became so great that she did not know what to do. Her husband filled his pockets and left for the next city, but he was never seen again. The giants cooked his bones over a pit of coal and the birds ate their fill of him. A young man found her in the tree, starving and half-mad with fear. Take aim with your gun and shoot into the middle of them, he said; take out the heart of the dead bird and swallow it whole.

Braking, jolting to a stop in front of the house, the incomprehensible woman untangles herself from the car and slams the door. She marches up to the crone who stands silently watching her from the front gate. The woman's voice shakes as she turns and points to the car where the faces of several children peer out anxiously. She pivots, angular and pale, focuses on the bundled things hanging from tall stakes in the yard, a profusion of weeds and broken glass. One of the children rolls down the car window to get a better look, his profile cropped in the side-view mirror, the skin under his eyes smudged blue with fatigue. Now the woman is squeezing her elbows, thoughts trailing. She won't look at the car. She can smell something like a swamp, only there's no water for miles around.

25.

His face is splotched with ruddy raised marks and his eyes are so light they are impossible to read. His men say he was splashed with acid by his own mother; others think it must have been a lover, but the thought of anyone undertaking that arrangement with him is almost too much to comprehend. He gives insane advice for common problems: a syringe of olive oil in the ear for a sore throat, a bath of mint and sand for lice, a song for the gangrened toes in their soaking boots. He stands over them while they sleep, arms crossed, a finger resting lightly on his lower lip. How they lie in formation, straight, narrow, blankets tucked in; it makes him feel something like pride. They find the letters the day he fails to return from patrol. His men read them aloud late into the night, one at a time, throwing chicken bones into the fire and wishing they were home.

My darling, I am mimicked all the time. My ears are full of mites and at night they move their limbs like whispering. We all have them and hear the sounds.

Walking straight through the fields now. The trees won't cover us. We still hear drones. We still have dry blankets.

It was beautiful because there was electricity. But something is wrong with the river. Something is keeping us from the dock.

26.

Tenderly the fox carried us in his jaws, set us inside his den, softened up the carrion for our supper; his wife sang us to sleep, a song for fattening up the hens in the henhouse: this is what all foxes dream of.

27.

At one time the grackles sang beautifully into the night like mockingbirds. It is said that the cries of the damned reach us through these birds now; that they were chosen for this duty because of their shiny black coats and piercing eyes; that it would have been the crows but they were already in the keep of witches. To this day grackles are wary and easily frightened, bearing their ugly voices like fists against the songbirds over the neighborhood maples and unnaturally green lawns.

28.

The old hare uses a cane to get anywhere. He tosses
a piece of fabric on his back to keep warm. He falls
repeatedly, each time feeling out in front of him for
the cane and hoisting himself back up. He barely
hears the crows that follow him all day. He remembers
outrunning dogs as the sun faded over the fields, the
many baby hares he has fathered. How in drought
years their tiny bodies were laid outside the dens like
offerings, while mother hares quivered below with
thirst and palsy.

29.

A couple stands at the edge of an insensible forest. They
are pale and stooped with sooty eyes and have walked a
long time. A russet-colored fox at their feet curls and
uncurls, its tail brushing their legs. Some sheep, skinny
coyotes, rabbits and moles and mice: all stop to rest in
and around the haggard man and woman. They sink to
their knees and the woman holds her hand out for the
mice but they keep the bread in their own mouths. The
man thinks of burial while the fox's head lolls back, and
the sheep marvel at the perfect cloven prints they have
made in the dry yellow grass.

GHOSTS

I am as cold as an ash-strewn stove in April. Afraid to land, birds endlessly circle. Car pulls alongside another car. Alone in the lake, brittle fingers tap the surface. A moon face drags weeds and swallows the lights below.

The ghost loves your sleeping self; so relaxed, your eyes sunk in a little, like the dead, your heart slow, hands curled under you like the fist of a doll.

2.

Has a bird ever flown too close to you? Perhaps you felt its wings beating furiously near your stomach; or beside your face, the shock and pulse of the air as it passed by. A bird may know a ghost but all they detect is a faint oval shape. As they fly they warp and swerve around these restless forms. The slightest sound like feathers pushing aside the atmosphere: all creatures of the spirit world emit a low hiss, as though air is being vacuumed into the spaces around them. Whatever else you read is merely speculation, or stories to scare children and old women.

A duplicate forest often emerges around a ghost, an imitation of leaf-light, birdsong, and sighing limbs. This doubling does not move a fox to anything more than passing curiosity. His body may twitch in recognition, but never in fear.

Ghosts despise the wind, for it feels like daggers to their already shredded and insubstantial bodies. As the old saying goes: A wind of great might chases a spirit in the night.

3.

She shudders along the roadside with her limbs
deciphered. You are close enough to hear them
clattering. A windshield held her indent but the driver
has already taken a sledgehammer to it: her backbone
a plaintiff pounded into dust. Her sightlines narrow
to a dreary hallway of open doors with see-saw voices
sobbing into amputated handkerchiefs.

4.

Wait for the crows over dark rows of corn. Wait for the farmer and his wife, who have forgotten the daylight and remember only dusk and deep night. They sleep all day and work by moonlight and stars, or by lamplight when clouds are thick in the midnight sky. Lonely spirits are drawn to the property, to the dim lights moving back and forth across the fields and in the barn, to hushed voices soothing wary cows and chickens. Owls share the rafters with shy ghosts, who peer into the gloom with faint memories of their own weight-bearing bodies.

5.

A ghost may easily inhabit the body of a bird or a rabbit, as an animal has no means of self-analysis: to dwell in the body of a person visits suffering upon a ghost because our souls weigh so heavily upon it. So the ghost will settle into the unfortunate creature and whisper from within: *Because your voice is not human, it cannot someday recite in low tones my weaknesses and imperfections into human ears.*

6.

People walk out of their homes in the morning and do not return. There is ferocity in these houses but no outward problem is evident. At night bands of gypsies and singers with guitars wander empty streets: voices and music ring out till dawn, pillaging the mayor's sleep. On these nights he looks through a box of old photos from his army days; their existence is the only proof of his life before he was thirty; the pictures are more appealing than the consequences of his memories. Cleanly broken bones were the pride of his battalion. Unsolved fingerprints smeared their woolen sweaters.

7.

Some say the goosanders who live in and around the shores nearby are the souls of settlers forced to swim across the river by their kidnappers. Their bodies were taken in pity and reborn as the birds.

Often one glimpses only the head of a waterbird bobbing in the river's current, its body beneath the water well hidden: seen in twilight, one could swear it was the head of a child.

8.

Grab the snout of a dog and the tip of his tail, then call out the name of your true love: she will appear in your dreams that night.

Tie an apron around the head of a horse at midnight on the new moon to summon and capture your true love's soul.

Hide your lover in a bale of straw. Cut her breath with a scythe and hang her in wire.

If the ghost of your true love appears at your window, cover your eyes with cotton and stay still until dawn. But if the ghost comes again the next night, you must lead her back to her jagged body in the cellar where she lies.

9.

The daughters of the house: the chimney sweep, covered in ashes: a ghost-face, smearing black marks on the furniture. Late that night he creeps back inside: sounds of sleeping, turning, blankets tucking under, a jaw clenched in a reticent dream. In the nanny's room he cuts her from ear to ear, swallows the jewels, wrings the cat's neck. He searches for the daughters in the darkness, but in each room finds nothing except the hint of recent breathing. Like a rampage, he grows with each lumbering step. Out in the garden his shadow cracks the flagstones as he bends into the well. The stone lions seem small when cupped in his hands.

10.

The slaughterhouse ghost clings to a fencepost beside a field in the dark. Over the field the black shape of faraway trees vaguely more defined than the black bowl of the sky. Before he was a ghost, he dreamt that he came upon such a field filled with cows, great lazy cows chewing and moving slowly in the grass. They would all turn and look at him at the same time, and that's when he would shout and raise his hand, and in an instant all the cows would crumple at once, dead on the ground, like a thousand bolts hit their brains in the same second; he would have the same dream with a field full of deer, would see the toothpick legs breaking and young velvet horns embedding in the dirt. Tonight the snow will drift through him, technicolor signals of deer and cows will play out over the black field, the dawn will come roughly and the wind will patiently carve him to pieces.

II.

Around you the women, golden, arms encircling. Are you weary? You'll pass through them, they'll bustle about, caring for your cavities, your brains and your bones. Passages inscribed on your arms, burned in with a match.

Swing your pall, wrap your hair in a bonnet, you are a giant, a cross hanging in the room above.

In truth, the rain will ruin the crops, but it plays like a low instrument before dawn, enhancing your sleep, veiling your ears of bell, buzzer, whining dog, angry wren. Rain arches your back, stains the foundation, fills in the pockets for the nestlings to sip, rushes you to school and train and ashcan garage of stolen radios. There's the popping of water upon pavement, green grass and leaves bouncing on each reedy stem.

12.

You carried your love this far: do not leave her in the field alone. There are long thin shadows cast by cattails, tiny snails mingle in the grass, dog prints in the mud—stay close. Above you, foul-hued clouds press about the roofs of houses. Silent gray doves turn their heads, thousands of shadows throbbing. Your throat tightens. The false whiteness of the moonlight is made up of many colors, just as there are many kinds of sleep.

CAPTIVES

I.

Another swamp, more flies, thousands of beetles pushing up, our feet and calves sinking and the howls of night birds. Sat on a bundle of dry rushes till daylight confessed, a fog shawled us through the morning. I can swear that I saw a woman hanging upside down from a great tree, can hold my hand to my heart and say she had no clothes, and my jaw shakes to remember it.

2.

We waited in a field beside a slice of the river. I dreamt
the field was rocks all of the same size and color,
dreamt spikes of black wood covering mud. Up to the
riverbank, as far as I could see, rocks and sticks and
mud. Trees and rushes gone. Something like frames
of houses, but blackened, rose up here and there: and
inside them lights—but not of lanterns and people—
only of fire and smoke. I dreamt of family walking on
the rocks and all were waving me to the fires.

3.

One of the girls returned to us but she cramped herself into the cellar. She looked across the river in summer and saw only a black web of branches and white snow down the rock face of the ridge. She said the leafless trees wrapped themselves together in fear, to wait for the time when the sun would disappear behind the low sloping mountain and never come back.

4.

A trio of girls walk the fringe of the parking lot, baskets of bread on each arm. Their clothes are dotted with stab holes from sharp pencils and old nails. They have no lace about their ears. Someone told them about birds hitting buildings, about dead birds by the thousands. The girls seek the graves of the birds whose bones are turning to coal. They place bottle caps in neat rows as markers for the remains, a sprinkle of crumbs for food in the afterlife. In dusty skin and solemn bowed heads are the cavities of lost bodies scored in the memory.

5.

A kilt or girdle, a twinflower bushel, a spade, a mirror:
such are the tools of the old women who live out by
the river. They stand by the water in the worst weather
to throw out their hexes and charms and don't feel the
sting of the townspeople on market day. Dead crows
and cats are bundled quietly, broken windows taped.
Obscenities coil into their hearts to drown and thrive
in the veins.

6.

One day in June all the baby starlings appeared, just like that: born of nothing but curses. *Hurrh-hurrh-hurrh* of their feeding throats drowns us out. Insect parts litter the streets, that white shit everywhere and dead robins too. The witches come out and stand on their front porches, clapping their hands to draw the starlings in for the night. Sickness has struck all over town, children falling one by one, their little organs gracefully shutting down, fevering away from consciousness. Mothers try clapping their hands but birds just hit the windows.

7.

Inside, we are perfectly absent of difference. Outside, we are creatures built like quilted skins. No stitch is the same; patterns overlap and pucker. I was once taken apart and remade as a hunter, but what kind of hunter am I? A map is creased into my cheeks, my ears are the whorls of a mountain, my crow's feet mark a small city. Wolves—standing on hind legs like circus animals, heads hidden by low-hanging branches—show me their overgrown claws and torn pads, tell me how each star sits alone in its own little chair.

8.

A waistband of leather and hooks, a waistband with a hatchet through it. A hatchet in an owl, feathers and dirt. Hatchet in the ice. We are a line in the snow and we crush a trail of prints. I see my arms lying in the snow. I see my sister in the river and I want to put my arms in the river. One man has his arms tied around a small tree and his hands are blue. I want to be an owl with the feathers of a mallard, greasy and warm. We are bowing like saplings; we are a border of cold bodies.

9.

A former spook forecast the ashes of sixteen John Does,
there was no blood when we flipped the body over, it
was so cold we held cigarette lighters under our mouths
to warm our tongues, we moved easily in the outbreak,
my terrier is shaking but there're no coyotes.

The bedspread is a polyester slide that administers oxygen. *This room is very clean,* I disclose to myself, but I forget and say it out loud. "Well. You ought to see the planes overhead," he says, "and you ought to put that voice of yours into the pillow."

II.

After weeks of overland travel and near-starvation, the captives were brought to a country crueler than most. They were left to wander the streets adrift, compelled by their weaknesses. Their scornful captors demanded information about the captives' government. Tell us what sort of ruler you serve, they prodded. If he is the most powerful, he must be bloody and cunning. The women of this new country held their heads delicately because of the bruising; with their mouths shut thin, it seemed they communicated only by gesture and side-eyed fluttering glances.

Several times a month a small group of young men would track down the captives and pick a fight with them—young men who were always stronger, faster, and more vicious than the previous pack of marauders. Convulsions bent the ones who were too hungry not to eat the scraps of rotted food left out by vaguely concerned passersby, and the newspapers reported the essential cowardice of this sickened and invisible citizenry.

They were put to the work of animals. The troublesome ones had pieces of their feet cut off to keep them close, like naked birds to the nest. Others were thrown from the riverbank into the water, where, among ice and sticks and thatches of plastic and weeds, they were tossed to the shallows. Stretched, sickle-bumped, raw-reddened, by now related to no species.

THE NEW WORLD

You can give one pound of body weight to the latitude of rejection, or body dysmorphic disorder, the capacity of brush-border, could we take a look at your files? Body of water straddles the boundary, peacock brought before the king, when we killed the females we recorded the following: body mass, gut morphology, small masses, peep toes, body odor, that minor cold turned to pneumonia. We dug a well in the bed of it, bulging.

NOTES

Grim was inspired by and modifies lines found in "The Pink Flower" and "Sweetheart Roland" from *The Complete Fairy Tales of the Brothers Grimm, Expanded Third Edition* (New York: Bantam, 2003).

"Each star sits alone in its own little chair" from "Inside, we are perfectly absent of difference..." is a line found in Grimm's "Seven Ravens" (Bantam, 2003).

"With this you'll be able to sew together..." uses and modifies lines found in Grimm's "The Four Skillful Brothers," "The Lazy Spinner," "The Iron Stove," "Faithful Ferdinand and Unfaithful Ferdinand," and "The Lettuce Donkey" (Bantam, 2003).

I also consulted *Favorite Fairy Tales Told in Poland* (Boston: Little, Brown, 1963), *Favorite Fairy Tales Told in Italy* (Boston: Little, Brown, 1965), and *English Fairy Tales* (New York: MacMillan, 1962).

Modified lines and words found in Fernando Pessoa's *The Book of Disquiet* (New York: Pantheon, 1991) appear in "You carried your love this far..." (*The Book of Disquiet*, entries 143 & 144; pp. 104–105) and in "A ghost may inhabit the body of a bird..." (*The Book of Disquiet*, entry 51; p. 36).

Some of the work found in *Captives* was inspired by the moving historical account of early New England in *The Unredeemed Captive* (New York: Vintage, 1995), by John Demos.

The pieces "The former spook…" and *The New World* were written partially by looking at the first few results of multiple Google searches created from random phrases. I would glance down the page of what Google returned and make quick notations of words or parts of sentences, some of which ended up in these pieces. I have since lost track of the various search terms and the exact sources of the text fragments I used here.

"Several times a month a small group of young men…" takes the phrase "invisible citizenry" from the book *Invisible Citizens: Captives and Their Consequences* (Salt Lake City: University of Utah Press, 2009), edited by Catherine M. Cameron.

ACKNOWLEDGMENTS

My thanks to the editors of the journals where some of these works (often in slightly different forms) first appeared: *Barrow Street*, *Bateau*, *Caketrain*, *Denver Quarterly*, *New South*, *Open Letters Monthly*, and *Society for Curious Thought*.

My gratitude to the following people who graciously helped me with this project along the way: Paige Ackerson-Kiely, John Cotter, Paul Fenouillet, Simon Marriott, Christian Peet, Josh Russell, Allison Titus, and Deb Olin Unferth; to Joshua Harmon, whose patience and encouragement know no end; and to my family, who helped me be an artist from the very beginning, but especially my mother, Faye McKenzie, and my father, Larry Goldstein, who tell the best stories.

ABOUT THE AUTHOR

Sarah Goldstein was born in Toronto and attended Concordia University (Montreal) and Cornell University. She currently resides in western Massachusetts. Her writing has appeared in *Barrow Street*, *Bateau*, *Caketrain*, *Denver Quarterly*, *New South*, *Verse*, and other journals, and her artwork has been shown in the US and Canada.

TARPAULIN SKY PRESS
Current & Forthcoming Titles

FULL-LENGTH BOOKS

Jenny Boully, *[one love affair]**

Jenny Boully, *not merely because of the unknown that was stalking toward them*

Ana Božičević, *Stars of the Night Commute*

Traci O Connor, *Recipes for Endangered Species*

Mark Cunningham, *Body Language*

Danielle Dutton, *Attempts at a Life*

Sarah Goldstein, *Fables*

Johannes Göransson, *Entrance to a colonial pageant in which we all begin to intricate*

Noah Eli Gordon & Joshua Marie Wilkinson, *Figures for a Darkroom Voice*

Gordon Massman, *The Essential Numbers 1991–2008*

Joyelle McSweeney, *Nylund, The Sarcographer*

Joanna Ruocco, *Man's Companions*

Kim Gek Lin Short, *The Bugging Watch & Other Exhibits*

Kim Gek Lin Short, *China Cowboy*

Shelly Taylor, *Black-Eyed Heifer*

Max Winter, *The Pictures*

Andrew Zornoza, *Where I Stay*

CHAPBOOKS

Sandy Florian, *32 Pedals and 47 Stops*
James Haug, *Scratch*
Paul McCormick, *The Exotic Moods of Les Baxter*
Teresa K. Miller, *Forever No Lo*
Jeanne Morel, *That Crossing Is Not Automatic*
Andrew Michael Roberts, *Give Up*
Brandon Shimoda, *The Inland Sea*
Chad Sweeney, *A Mirror to Shatter the Hammer*
Emily Toder, *Brushes With*
G.C. Waldrep, *One Way No Exit*

&

Tarpaulin Sky Literary Journal
in print and online
www.tarpaulinsky.com